DISNEP · PIXAR

SOUL

Adapted by
Courtney Carbone

Illustrated by
Sophia Lin and **Nick Balian**

Designed by
Tony Fejeran

A GOLDEN BOOK · NEW YORK

© 2020 Disney Enterprises, Inc. and Pixar. All rights reserved. Published in the United States
by Golden Books, an imprint of Random House Children's Books, a division of Penguin
Random House LLC, 1745 Broadway, New York, NY 10019, and in Canada by Penguin
Random House Canada Limited, Toronto, in conjunction with Disney Enterprises, Inc. Golden
Books, A Golden Book, A Little Golden Book, the G colophon, and the distinctive gold spine
are registered trademarks of Penguin Random House LLC.
rhcbooks.com
ISBN 978-0-7364-4074-5 (trade) — ISBN 978-0-7364-4075-2 (ebook)
Printed in the United States of America
10 9 8 7 6 5 4 3 2 1

Joe Gardner was a middle-school band teacher. But his real dream was to become a **professional jazz musician**. He knew it was what he was born to do!

One day, Joe got a call from **Curley Baker**, an old student of his. Curley invited Joe to audition for the famous **Dorothea Williams Quartet**. They were playing at **The Half Note**, a legendary jazz club.

At the audition, Joe's fingers **flew across** the piano keys. Dorothea was **impressed** with Joe's performance.

She told Joe to find a good suit for the show later that night.

Joe's dream was finally coming true! He called everyone he knew, eager to **share the good news**.

Joe was so **distracted** . . .

. . . that he fell into an **uncovered manhole**!

The next thing Joe knew, he had taken the form of a soul on a moving sidewalk heading toward a bright light. Glowing souls around him said they were going to The Great Beyond. Joe did not like the sound of that! He ripped through a barrier and fell

down,
down,
down...

. . . into the **You Seminar**, where new souls prepared for life on Earth. Here they would get their personalities and find one last special thing—their **Spark**.

A soul counselor named **Jerry** thought Joe
was a lost mentor. Mentors helped new souls
find their Spark!

Joe was paired with a new soul named **22**.
But 22 had been paired with hundreds of mentors
before. She didn't want to go to Earth!

Joe and 22 visited a room filled with Joe's **ordinary memories**. Joe admitted that he wasn't a mentor. He just wanted to get back to his life on Earth and perform with Dorothea Williams.

Joe wasn't like any mentor 22 had had before. She told Joe he could go to Earth **in her place**!

But first, Joe had to help 22 find her Spark so she could earn her Earth Pass and give it to him. Joe thought finding 22's purpose on Earth would help her find her Spark.

22 experimented with **baking** . . .

chemistry . . .

and **firefighting**.

Then she tried being an **astronaut** . . .

a **librarian** . . .

and even **president**.

Dozens of tries later, 22 still had not found her Spark.
And they were **out of time**!

22 had an idea. She led Joe through a portal to the Astral Plane. There, they met a mystic named **Moonwind**, who helped Joe find his body in a hospital on Earth.

But there was a terrible **mix-up**— 22 entered Joe's body, and Joe ended up in the body of Mr. Mittens, the hospital therapy cat!

Joe and 22 escaped from the hospital and discovered themselves on the **noisy streets of New York City!**

Luckily, they found Moonwind on a street corner. He told them to meet him later at The Half Note to get Joe back into his body.

While they waited, Joe and 22 spent the day preparing for Joe's show. 22 had to pretend to be Joe—and for the first time, 22 saw how **wonderful** life could be.

As the day ended, 22 thought she might be ready to stay on Earth. But Joe disagreed. He didn't think she was ready. Besides, Joe needed his body back—*now*.

But 22 refused to give up Joe's body. Suddenly, a portal appeared and transported them both to the You Seminar. Someone had tracked Joe down on Earth!

The counselors were **shocked** to learn that 22 had finally earned her Earth Pass! But Joe believed she had only earned it because she'd pretended to be him. 22 gave Joe her Earth Pass and disappeared.

Joe returned to Earth just in time for the show. The **crowd went wild** as Joe played. It was everything he'd ever wanted—and then it was over.

He'd thought he would feel different after the show, but **everything was the same**.

Back at home, Joe sat at his piano and thought of the small, special moments of his day with 22. As Joe played, he traveled back to the Astral Plane.

Moonwind met Joe there with terrible news: 22 had become a **lost soul**! They tried to catch her in Moonwind's boat, but 22 escaped to the You Seminar.

Joe chased 22 as she tore through the You Seminar, leaving **destruction** in her wake.

Finally, Joe cornered 22 at the edge of the Earth Portal.
He tried to apologize for telling her she wasn't ready to go
to Earth. But just when he thought 22 was listening,
she swallowed him whole.

Inside the lost soul, Joe found the real 22, upset and scared. He gently handed her a small **seedpod** she'd collected during their day together, and the storm began to calm.

Joe told 22 he used to think that finding your Spark was about realizing your purpose, but now he knew it was really about being **inspired by life**. 22 was ready after all.

Joe gave the Earth Pass to 22, and together, the two friends **jumped toward Earth**. At the last moment, Joe was **taken back** to The Great Beyond, but 22 continued, eager to explore the world on her own.

On the moving sidewalk, the counselor had **a gift for Joe**. It was a special Earth Portal just for him! Joe had inspired all the counselors by helping 22, and they wanted to thank him. With just one step, Joe entered the portal, ready to **appreciate** every moment of his life.